Waiting for Snow

Illustrations: Jenny Williams
Text: Jonathan Shipton

Concept, creation and design FBA Publications in association with the
Qualifications, Curriculum & Assessment Authority (ACCAC)
FBA Publications
Aberystwyth
1999

'Where's my reading book, Mam?' asked Gareth.
'Has anyone seen my red hair-band?' yelled Bethan.
It was a cold morning in January.
The grass in the garden was frosty white.
But Gareth didn't want to wear his coat.
And he definitely didn't want to wear gloves!
'Come on,' said Mrs Roberts, 'Mrs Patel and Amin
are waiting and I'm late for work!'

As they left the house Gareth spotted some icicles.
He broke one off.
It looked like a lolly ... but it tasted horrible!
Gareth ran after his sister.
'Look! Bethan, I've got a lovely surprise for you!'
But Bethan didn't want the surprise.
And neither did their friend Amin!

When they arrived at school, there was a crowd
of people waiting outside the gate.
'I wonder what's going on,' said Amin's mum.
Bethan's teacher was talking to some of the parents.
The central heating had broken down and school
was closed until Monday.

4

5

'I know what we'll do,' said Mrs Patel. 'We'll catch the bus into town and call in to see your mother at work in the supermarket.'
The shops in Llanelli were very busy - and so was Mrs Roberts on the check-out till. She was very surprised to see them there!
'We're going to play at Amin's this afternoon,' Bethan told her mam.

Later, after hot soup at Amin's house
they all went down to the park to play.
There was a family of ducks sitting on the ice.
'Poor things,' said Bethan. 'I wish we had some food to give them.'
Gareth dived into his coat pocket and pulled out an old packet of crisps.
They were all scrunched up but luckily the ducks didn't mind.
'Time we were getting back,' said Mrs Patel, looking at her watch.
'It's four o'clock and getting dark already.'

SANDY WATER PARK
PARC DŴR SANDY

7

After tea they watched the news.
There were pictures of the bad weather from all over the British Isles.
There were villages cut off by the snow in the north.
There were lorries stuck on motorways in the east.
There were children sledging in the south, but there was no snow in the west for Wales.
'It's not fair!' moaned the children.
'Where's our snow?'
'I expect it's got lost in the mountains!' laughed Mrs Patel.

8

Later on, when Gareth and Bethan were back
at home, they watched the weather forecast.
There were snow symbols appearing all over the map.
'Oh no!' said Gareth,
'She's going to run out before she gets to us!'
But she didn't.
One fat snowflake ended up just above Llanelli!
Winter was here at last!

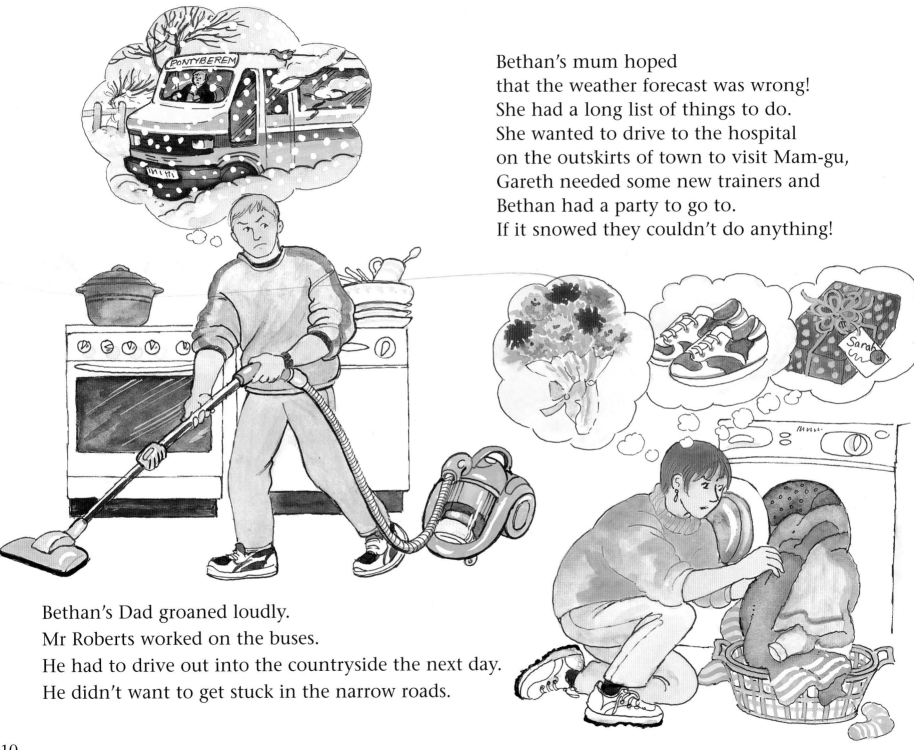

Bethan's mum hoped
that the weather forecast was wrong!
She had a long list of things to do.
She wanted to drive to the hospital
on the outskirts of town to visit Mam-gu,
Gareth needed some new trainers and
Bethan had a party to go to.
If it snowed they couldn't do anything!

Bethan's Dad groaned loudly.
Mr Roberts worked on the buses.
He had to drive out into the countryside the next day.
He didn't want to get stuck in the narrow roads.

Bethan and Gareth woke up very early the next day.
There was no snow anywhere!
'It's not fair!' said Gareth to his dad.
Mr Roberts looked up at the heavy yellow sky.
'Don't worry,' he said. 'I'm sure it's on its way!'

On the way to the hospital they went to the
market to buy a treat for Mam-gu.
'These grapes look juicy,' said Bethan.
'I like chocolates better!' announced Gareth.

When they arrived at the hospital the car park was full.
Mrs Roberts had to drive round and round looking for a space.
There was an ambulance waiting by the entrance.
Its lights were flashing and the back doors were wide open.
Bethan and Gareth peeped inside but it was empty.

'How do we find Mam-gu?' said Bethan.
'Easy peasy!' said Gareth. 'Look at the plan. Follow me!'
Before anyone could stop him Gareth darted off to the right.

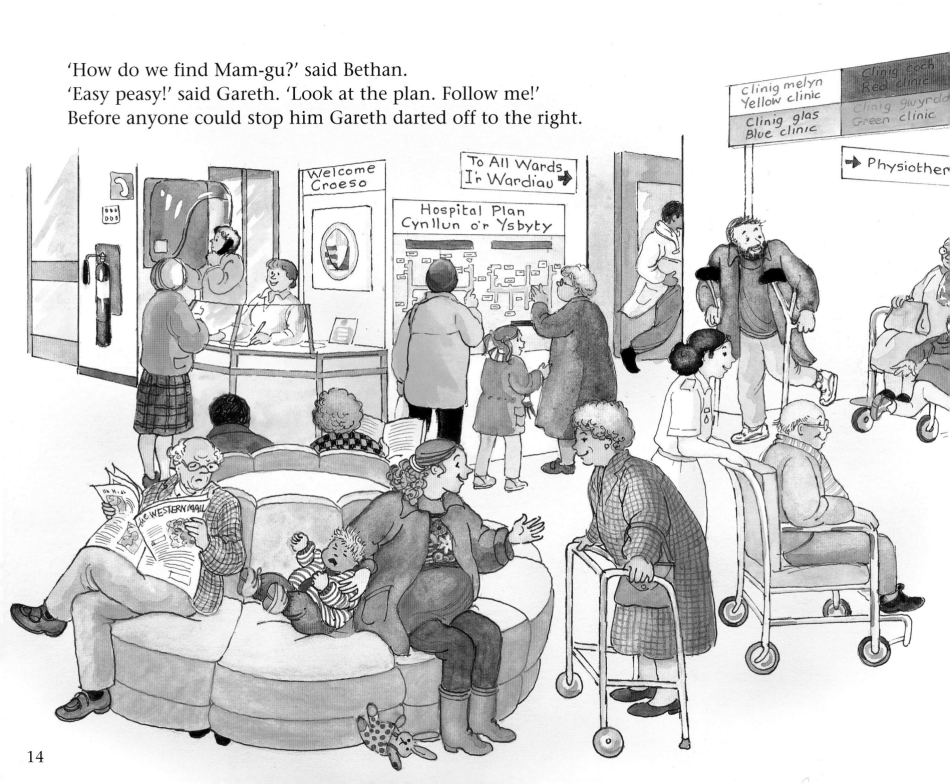

WARD 3

Bethan and her mum followed the directions to
Mam-gu's ward - left first, up the stairs and then right.
When they arrived Mam-gu was sitting up in bed.
She was talking to a nurse.
But where was Gareth?
'I don't believe it!' exclaimed Mrs Roberts. 'He's lost!'

15

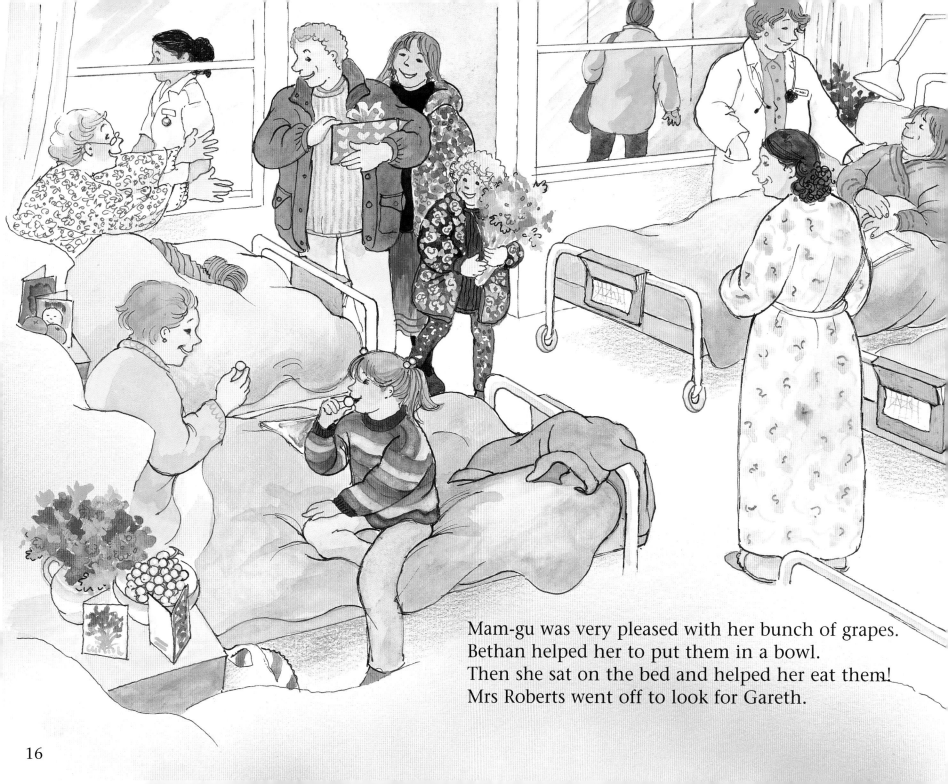

Mam-gu was very pleased with her bunch of grapes.
Bethan helped her to put them in a bowl.
Then she sat on the bed and helped her eat them!
Mrs Roberts went off to look for Gareth.

16

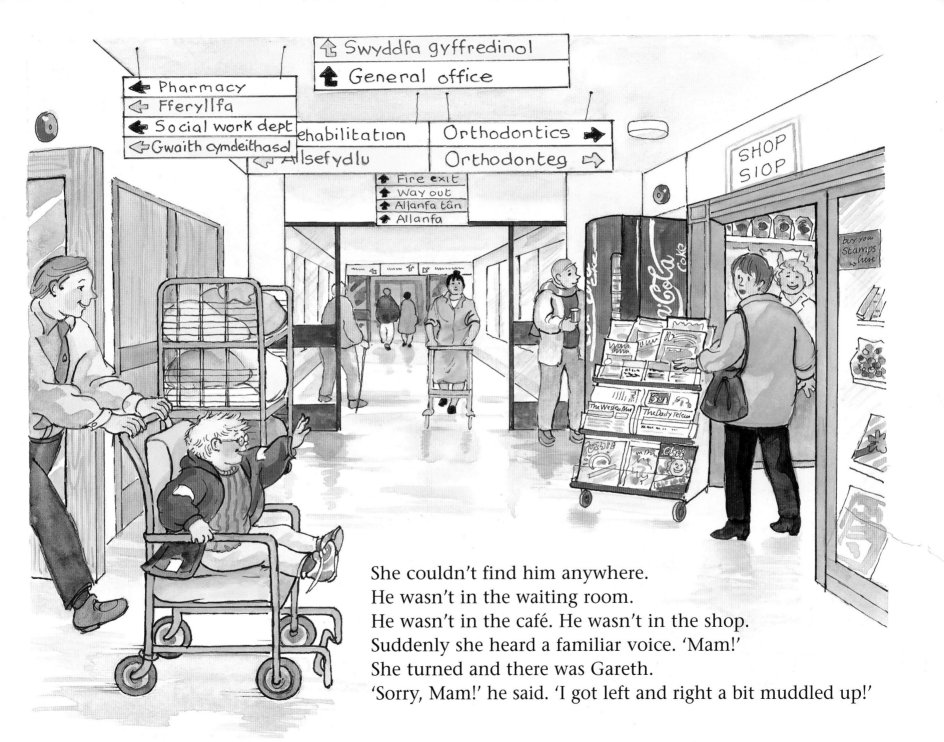

She couldn't find him anywhere.
He wasn't in the waiting room.
He wasn't in the café. He wasn't in the shop.
Suddenly she heard a familiar voice. 'Mam!'
She turned and there was Gareth.
'Sorry, Mam!' he said. 'I got left and right a bit muddled up!'

By the time they reached the shopping centre, the sky was quite dark.
By the time they had finished their pizza, it was snowing!
The two children rushed outside.
They wanted to play.
But Gareth had to have his new trainers ...

Mrs Roberts drove very carefully on the way home.
The roads were slippery and it was difficult to see.
'I hope Dad's bus isn't stuck in a snowdrift,' said Bethan.
'So do I!' replied their mum.

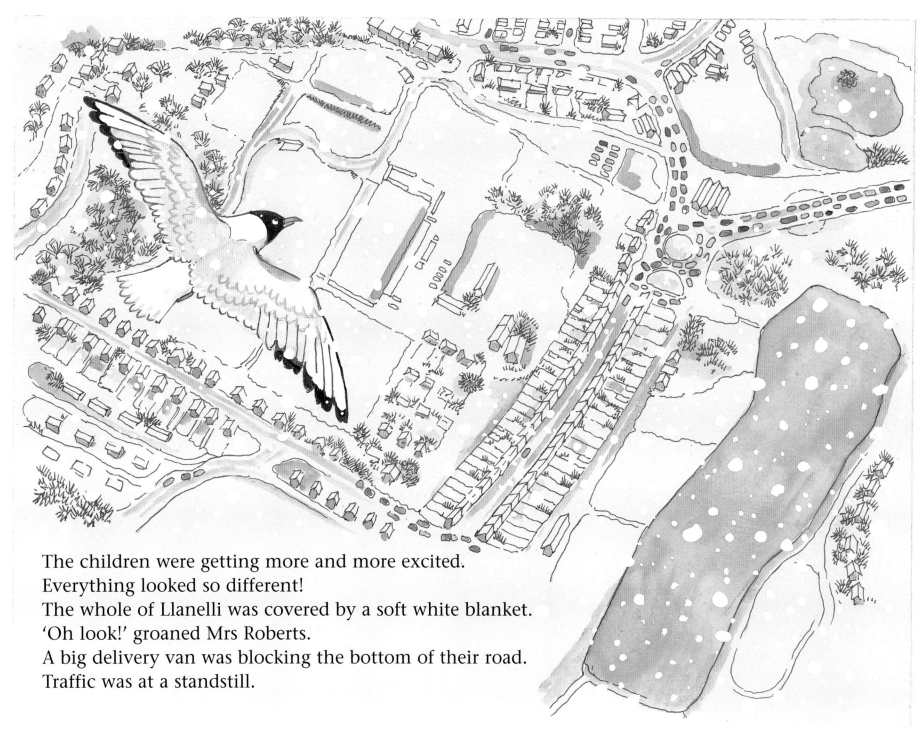

The children were getting more and more excited.
Everything looked so different!
The whole of Llanelli was covered by a soft white blanket.
'Oh look!' groaned Mrs Roberts.
A big delivery van was blocking the bottom of their road.
Traffic was at a standstill.

They had to leave the car and walk home with their shopping.
'Great!' said Gareth, 'Dad's here!'
Mr Roberts had come home early because of the bad weather.
'I don't like this snow,' said Bethan. 'I can't go to the party.'
'Well ... we certainly can't go in the car,' said Mrs Roberts.
'But don't worry. We'll get you there somehow!'

And they did!

PARTY HERE

23

British Library Cataloguing-in-Publication Data

A catalogue record for this publication is available from the
British Library

Published with the financial assistance of ACCAC (The Qualifications,
Curriculum & Assessment Authority for Wales)

Published May 1999 by
FBA Publications, Number 4, The Science Park
Aberystwyth, Ceredigion SY23 3AH
Tel: (01970) 611996 Fax: (01970) 625796
Email: publishing@fba.wales.com

Designed by Francis Balsom Associates
Edited by Priscilla Gibby
Printed in Wales

ISBN 1 901862 32 1